Giftwright Book Four

The Glass Hatchet

Karine Green

Staunton Press

The Giftwright's Workshop: Book Four

The Glass Hatchet

ASIN B0GY1GBB9M

Print ISBN: 978-1-972492-06-2

Imprint: Staunton Press

Staunton Press – Tampa Florida

First Edition: May 2026

Cover design by Karine Green

Contents

There are five books in this series. This is book Two: The Glass Slippers

"The Giftwright" Welcome to the Giftwright's Workshop, where fairy tales are remade through the lens of magical craftsmanship. These five interconnected stories shift focus from princes and ballrooms to the workshop that makes magic possible, and the hands that shape memory, protection, and penance into glass.

"The Glass Slipper" A retelling of Cinderella. What does it mean to craft something meant to be seen but not kept? How do you bind protection into glass as fragile as a promise, knowing it must withstand a night of dancing? And what happens when a glassblower and a cobbler with entirely different kinds of magic must collaborate to create shoes that will walk away on someone else's feet?

"The Glass Rose" A retelling of Beauty and the Beast, where the enchanted rose becomes an engineering challenge. How do you preserve a curse in glass, giving someone time to break it themselves? Can a rose dome hold dark magic at bay long enough for love to break what enchantment began?

"The Glass Hatchet" A retelling of the European folk tale "The Glass Axe," exploring grief, protective love, and the cost of penance. In the original, a cursed prince must complete impossible tasks with fragile glass tools. Here we ask: what if the glass hatchet was meant to protect rather than harm? What if the solution wasn't escape, but acknowledgment of debt? Like all tales in the Giftwright collection, this story examines how magical craftsmen navigate the space between what clients ask for and what they truly need, and what happens when fragile things break

GIFTWRIGHT BOOK FOUR

"The Glass Ring" bringing together everything Neve has learned about the space between what clients ask for and what they do with the aftermath someone else left them with. Some commissions require more than craft; they require understanding that fragile things break, and sometimes that breaking is exactly what's needed.

This is where it all begins. Welcome to the Giftwright's workshop

CHAPTER ONE

The Commission

Winter, Second Year

The workshop smelled of argent twine and cooling glass. Neve was shaping a memory vessel for a merchant's widow when the bell above the door rang.

Mira moved closer to the counter. She set down her charcoal, brushed the dust from her fingers, and looked up. "Good morning. Welcome to the Giftwright Workshop."

"Good morning." The visitor's voice was low and pleasant. "What a remarkable shop. I had heard about your reputation, of course, but reputation rarely does justice to the real thing."

Neve looked up. Flattery came in two kinds. The excessive sort that wanted discounts, and the observational sort from someone who genuinely knew what they were looking at.

The woman at the counter was probably around forty, with dark hair streaked with silver, neatly pinned back. She wore a deep gray traveling cloak, weathered but intact, showing signs of real exposure. To Neve, she resembled a member of the Fairy Godparents' Guild. Her eyes moved around the workshop, glancing at the cooling rack, the annealing oven, and the pipes lined up by size along the wall. She noticed the mask on Neve's face and offered a small nod.

At the bench by the window, Hollis sat with his hands folded in his lap. He hadn't operated the furnace in three weeks. His cough had worsened throughout December and into the new year. On mornings when the cold was sharp off the river, he sometimes didn't come downstairs until midday. But now he was here, watching the visitor with pale gray eyes that missed nothing.

"Master Hollis." The woman turned to him with a slight incline of her head. "Your ornament work saved my colleague's grandmother's Christmas memory twelve years ago. It still glows perfectly."

Hollis's expression did not change. "What colleague?"

"Mafalda. Of the Fairy Godparents Guild." She smiled. "I am Sylvaine. I work in the eastern districts, a different specialty from Mafalda, but we consult regularly. She speaks very highly of this workshop." She turned to Neve. "The glass slippers were exceptionally clever work."

Neve pulled down his mask. "What can we help you with?"

"A commission." She placed a folded paper on the counter. "A glass hatchet. I need it to hold a safety ward bound to a child. The boy is eleven years old and has a gift for woodland magic that needs channeling before it becomes dangerous to him. His family has agreed to the arrangement. The ward would allow him to practice woodcraft safely, chopping kindling and learning the craft, with the protection ensuring that no accident can harm him while he learns. I brought the supplies, so it shouldn't strain your shop."

She handed Neve a piece of parchment and then laid out argent twine that sparkled with golden dust.

"It's his mother's wedding ring, melted and dusted down. We coated the argent twine in it to bind her protection over him."

Neve took the paper and unfolded it. The specifications were precise: dimensions, weight distribution, handle length scaled for a child's grip, and blade geometry. Whoever had written this understood how a tool was actually used by small hands not yet sure of themselves.

"You want the ward bound to the hatchet rather than the boy," Neve said, concerned that this woman hadn't considered one of the most important facts about using a glass anything to impact wood. "If a fairy godmother can't protect him, what is after him?"

"It's meant to fill in where I can't. Bound to the hatchet and keyed to him. So it only functions in his hands." Sylvaine folded her hands on the counter. "His family is cautious. They wanted the protection to be specific. The mother is out of the picture, so this is to protect against any future stepparents."

"That's sensible." Neve glanced at Hollis, who gave the smallest nod. "The glasswork is the challenge. A hatchet needs to absorb impact repeatedly. Memory glass is built to preserve, not endure the force of chopping wood."

The impact-resistant rose case must be making its way through the gossip channels. While he could make glass strong, it was still glass. It would shatter if someone tried to use it as an hatchet.

"I know. That is precisely why I came here rather than anywhere else." She paused. "I understand your apprentice has some background in materials that bear weight under repeated stress."

Mira was already studying the specifications over Neve's shoulder. "Cobbler work. Magical reinforcement for mining boots mostly. I have been learning how to apply those principles to glass."

"Then you understand exactly what I need." Sylvaine's attention moved back to Neve. "A tool that holds enchantment without sacrificing function."

Neve looked at the blade geometry again. Thinner at the edge than he would have chosen for durability alone, but the thinness was probably intentional so the warding enchantment could concentrate correctly at the point of contact. He thought about argent twine weave running through an object meant to strike rather than sit. The problem was interesting. A glass hatchet that could actually be used as a hatchet, that could hold a child's ward without shattering on first contact with a log. Hollis would have called it impossible right up until it wasn't.

"The ward," Neve said. "I need the exact terms. What I am binding shapes how I build the glass around it."

"Safety from accidental harm during woodcraft practice," Sylvaine said. "The boy cannot injure himself with the hatchet while he holds it, and no falling branch or timber can strike him while the ward is active as he learns his trade. Of course, the other protections will be inherent to the potion-treated argent twine."

"Duration?"

"Indefinite. As long as the glass holds."

"How often will he use it?"

"Once a month. His family believes in earning skill rather than relying on magic." She paused. "They do not want him swinging it daily and learning to depend on the protection instead of his own judgment."

Neve wrote that into his notes. Monthly use. One session per month. He was thinking about impact cycles and stress distribution and how many blows per session a child would realistically manage, and the answer she had given satisfied the question he had asked.

"How much were you looking to spend?" he said.

She smiled. "Two thousand gold crowns. Half now, half upon completion."

More than generous for a single commission.

"Two thousand crowns?" Mira looked suspiciously at her.

Neve nodded. "That's very generous, but also high."

"This is the only son of the couple. If anything happens to him, it'll destroy the boy's father. He's willing to make sure the best is commissioned for this job." Sylvaine smiled, pleasantly. "The loss of a parent, the grief of that loss, isn't something even the best fairy godparent can protect a child from. I can only protect him from further injuring himself. His magic is coming in a bit wild. His father has important work to do for the realm, so he can't always be there."

"Four days," Neve said. "I want to test impact resistance before I call it finished."

"Four days is perfectly acceptable. We can test it. Its properties are only bound to the boy. You could break it." Sylvaine set a leather purse on the counter. She reached into her cloak and produced a small, waxed packet. "The boy's hair for the binding."

Neve picked it up. One strand, fine and dark.

"His name," Neve said. "The binding anchors better to a person than to hair alone. And I should be able to test it as the manufacturer. I would have full access to any of the magic here, the same as the person it was intended for."

"Emory," Sylvaine said. "His name is Emory, and isn't the hair part of him? And it's fine. I can test it. I promise."

Neve nodded. "Yes, but this is magical glass, combined with potions. As you know, magic requires intent. I will need to infuse intent into it, or there will be nothing magical about it. It simply won't activate the potions. You are here to purchase magical glass, not just a glass hatchet. Unless I'm mistaken about your request?"

Mira leaned in next to Neve. "We understand that fairy godparents and some higher-performing wizards have extraordinary, all-encompassing magical abilities, but this is a magical craft. We have more focused and potent magical abilities that must be channeled into this. It's not as simple as waving a wand and saying a spell, not that we could do that. Our essence is actually infused with this, along with the potion making."

She smiled, "Yes, of course. Magic does have a way of balancing the power, doesn't it?"

He wasn't sure he liked this woman. However, two thousand crowns was something the shop needed. And if it could help the boy even better.

Neve wrote it in the commission ledger. Date, name, specifications, fee paid. Below the entry he added a note in smaller letters: *Verify: Sylvaine, eastern districts, FGP Guild. Mafalda referral.*

He had learned that from Hollis. Verify ward referrals. Always.

Sylvaine moved through the workshop without hurry. She paused at the annealing oven and asked, "Does the cooling rate change when glass is carrying magical wards or is it the same as regular glass?"

Neve shrugged, "Mostly it's the same. The only ones that took longer were the glass slippers you mentioned. This will probably take a little bit longer because of the strengthening wards. It's going to be very similar to the slippers because we're going to have to add the impact resistance potions to it; otherwise, it's going to shatter on the first hit."

She nodded, moving on to the next item in the shop, pausing again at the memory vessel Mira had finished the previous afternoon, studied the argent twine pattern for a moment, and said, "That's a tighter weave than I've seen before. Whose design?"

"Mine," Mira told her. "It's for keeping potion flowers fresher longer. The apothecary has an order outstanding for them."

"It's beautiful. Do you sell them individually?" Sylvaine nodded as if filing it away.

"Yes, This one is for home use. It's twenty-five crowns, but it'll last a lifetime if cared for properly," Mira said, smiling.

"Can I have one with the dotted swirls? Like this." She pointed to another piece.

"I'll have it ready for delivery when you pick up the hatchet." Mira smiled. Neve knew there was a lot of satisfaction behind it. He and Hollis had been skeptical of adding the piece, but so far it was a money spinner.

She thanked all three of them, pulled her cloak close against the winter air in the doorway, and left.

The bell chimed.

Neve stood looking at the commission ledger.

"I'll send word to Mafalda today," he said. "Confirm the referral before we begin."

"Good," Hollis said. "I have not seen her around before, but if she's in the Eastern Division, that could explain it."

He was still watching the door, hands folded in his lap. His face had gone still, as if something were unsettling him. "She knew exactly how the ward needed to be structured. The binding specifications, the keying to the child, the indefinite duration, the monthly interval. Most clients know what they want. They don't know the mechanics of how it works. She knows a lot about magical glass for someone who doesn't work with it."

"She's guild," Neve said. "She's seen it done. Mafalda's never made glass before, but she can probably explain the basics."

"That makes sense." Hollis picked up a length of argent twine from the bench beside him and turned it between his fingers. "Send the message today, Neve. Before you heat the first gather."

"I said I would," Neve said patiently.

"I know you did."

He said nothing else. Neve sent the message to Mafalda before the furnace reached working temperature, then put his mask on and began the preliminary shaping. Mira settled at the bench with parchment and charcoal and worked out the load-bearing angles.

"The blade needs a thicker spine," she said, not looking up. "The edge can stay thin for the enchantment, but a narrow spine will crack on the second or third blow regardless of reinforcement." She turned the parchment toward him. "Here."

He looked at her sketch and nodded. "Yes. Exactly like that."

They did not hear back from Mafalda that day.

Neve figured she was busy. He worked on the preliminary shaping, let Mira's structural notes guide his choices, and considered the problem of making glass withstand repeated impacts from a child's hands. Good work. Interesting work. It wouldn't work if an adult tried to chop wood with it, but small hands wouldn't have that much chopping power.

They did not hear from Mafalda the following day either.

On the third day, Neve finished the hatchet in the late afternoon. It sat on the cooling rack as the low winter sun came through the workshop windows, translucent and sharp, the argent twine woven through its spine in the pattern Mira had designed. The ward was bound cleanly into the glass, anchored to the strand of hair, keyed to the name Emory. The reinforcement would distribute impact the way

Mira's mining boots distributed weight through stone and clay.

It was some of the finest work they had ever done as a collaboration.

Hollis came, stood beside him, and looked at it without speaking. After a moment, he nodded and went back to his chair.

Mira smiled as she prepared the box for the potion flower pot for travel.

Sylvaine collected the hatchet and the pot the following morning, arriving at opening time. She set the remaining payment on the counter without being asked, coins already separated, exact to the figure. Then she unwrapped the velvet covering and held the hatchet up to the light, and the argent twine threw small points of brightness across the workshop ceiling.

“Wow, this is beautiful,” she said, focusing on the pot.

"We've never sent out work untested," Neve said, starting to worry.

“Surely this has been.” She pointed at the pot.

"I mean this." He held up the hatchet. "You should keep the wrapping on it to keep the ward bound only to the boy. It follows the first touch rule, meaning the first one who touches it basically owns its protections and will not work for another."

"Extraordinary," she said. Her voice was entirely sincere. "We'll test it, but I am sure there won't be an issue."

"The reinforcement runs the full length of the spine," Neve said. "Once it's tested, let me know. I want to know if anything needs adjustment."

"I will." She carefully wrapped the hatchet, thanked him, and left with the pot in the box under her arm.

The bell chimed.

Mafalda's reply arrived two hours later, carried by a folded, paper bird that came through the ventilation gap above the workshop door and dropped onto the bench in front of Neve. He recognized the fold. Urgent guild correspondence stamped on its wing.

He unfolded it.

Neve. Tell me immediately that you did not accept a commission from a woman named Sylvaine claiming to represent the Fairy Godparents Guild. Tell me you have not given her anything. She was expelled from this guild fourteen months ago for the deliberate cursing of her own fairy godchild, a boy named Emory, eleven years old. I testified at the expulsion hearing myself. I am in the middle of a complicated matter. A princess, a cursed spinning wheel, a household that has not listened to a word of good advice in three generations. I cannot come immediately. But I am coming. Do nothing until I arrive.

Neve read it twice. Then a third time, trying to push the growing sense of dread down.

The name Emory sat in his commission ledger in his own handwriting like a knife in his chest.

Neve's only saving grace was that he had manufactured protection into the hatchet. Emory could not injure himself with the hatchet while he holds it. He shuddered at the thought of what might actually be chopped if he had skipped that step.

The hatchet could only chop wood.

Once a month. That's only one log, so half an hour at the most.

As long as the glass holds. He cringed. What would happen if the glass broke?

He set the letter down on the bench. His hands were steady. The furnace hissed in the background, patient and indifferent.

Hollis had come to the bench. His gaze settled on the note. "Mafalda."

"Her reply came." Neve picked up the letter and read it aloud. His voice stayed level. The workshop was quiet around the words.

When he finished, Mira set down the pipe she had been warming. She looked at Neve and said nothing, only covering her mouth as if what she was thinking was unspeakable.

Hollis turned and sat in his chair for a long moment. "She had everything planned before she walked through that door. The fake referral. The name. The hair. The specifications were written so that every word was true, and none of it was what it appeared to be." He coughed into his sleeve. "She knew you would verify. She knew what the delay would be. She timed the collection before the reply could arrive, I'll bet, because she knew we couldn't reach Mafalda until it was too late."

“Are we sure she was Fairy Godparent Guild and not a genie?” Mira asked, looking confused. “Who would do that, if not a genie?”

“Former fairy godparent, according to Mafalda.” Neve let out a slow breath. "She brought us cursed ingredients to use, because she knew we didn't have enough magic to figure it out."

"Do you think so? She seemed unaware of the different levels," Mira asked.

“She was faking, and I agree with Hollis. I wouldn’t be surprised if she did cause the crisis that pulled guild members away, knowing the verification, or lack thereof, wouldn’t arrive until it was too late,” Neve said, feeling disgusted with himself. “It’s why we work in magical trades and not the upper magical guilds.”

"Right now, I would be more surprised if she didn't. The heat of the glass would melt the silver and gold together, completing whatever curse she'd laid on them." Hollis said.

Neve looked at the commission ledger again. At the name Emory. "The real question is, what have I done?"

Not a question.

"Send for Mafalda. Tell her it's an emergency," Hollis said. "Now. Then we come up with a plan."

Neve was already writing the response, glad that Mira had the magic to send the paper bird back to Mafalda.

CHAPTER TWO

The Furnace

Three days later, Neve had just set down his pen when the workshop door opened.

The man who came in was perhaps forty-five, road dust on his boots and coat, dark circles under his eyes that went beyond one bad night. Behind him, a boy came through the door with a split log tied around his waist, and a glass hatchet firmly gripped in his hands.

The boy was small. Eleven, from the height of him, though exhaustion had made him look younger. He moved to the nearest wall and stood with his back against it. His body shuddered and the hatchet came down against the log. A few pale threads of wood curled to the floor. He did not look at the blade or the wood. He stared at nothing while his arms rose and fell again, and the sound of each tiny strike was barely louder than a breath.

Neve looked at the hatchet. His own argent twine work caught the morning light. His mark was on the handle, small and precise.

He came around the counter. Not toward the man. Toward the boy.

"You made this." The man's voice was worn to flatness, past anger into the country beyond it. "There is a mark on the handle. I had a craftsman in this city examine it two days ago. He said the mark belongs to the Giftwright Workshop here in Silverneve."

Neve crouched so he was level with the boy. Exhausted eyes, wary but present. "May I see it?"

"I can't put it down," the boy said. His voice came out thin with use. "It won't let me."

"I know. May I take it from you? I am the manufacturer; my magic was used. I should be able to take it."

The boy looked at his outstretched hands for a moment. Then he held the hatchet out.

Neve took it.

It released cleanly from the boy's grip, the way glass recognizes the hand that shaped it. Neve felt his mark under his fingers, the warmth of his own work, and then the compulsion hit him.

His other hand compulsively gripped the hatchet, and his arms came down.

The hatchet struck the log. It was all he could do to keep the full force of a blow from happening.

A pale shaving curled to the floor. He breathed a sigh of relief, the glass held.

Neve looked at his own hand. It rose again, slowly, with the patient inevitability of a tide. He set his jaw and held it. The compulsion pushed. He pushed back. It was like holding a door against something that did not tire as it pushed to get in.

"Neve," Mira said, reaching toward him.

"I have it," he said.

His arms came down again. Another tiny shaving. The sound was nearly nothing, glass against grain, a whisper.

Mira came forward. Her fingers closed around the handle above his and held for a moment, and then something in the glass simply denied her. Not a push.

More as if her hand had forgotten it was holding anything at all. She tried again with both hands. The same result.

Hollis rose from his chair. He crossed the workshop at the careful pace his lungs required these days and wrapped both hands around the hatchet. The same thing happened. His hands opened. He stepped back.

“And what makes you think we haven’t already tried that!” The man bellowed. “Do you not know the meaning of a cursed object?”

"Right," Hollis said. He looked at the man by the door. "Sit down. Tell us everything."

“I am Lord Aldric Regentry,” he said, glaring at them. “This is my son, Emory.” He pointed to the boy as tears ran down his face. “Why have you done this? What harm have we caused you? That you would curse my son? My only heir. This isn’t about the negotiations with your brother, the Duke of Silverneve?”

Neve shook his head. “Trust me, if Duke Garrett Silverneve had an issue, he would have no problem saying so.”

Aldric sat. He pulled his hat from his head and turned it in his hands.

"Three days ago." He stopped. Started again. "A woman came to the door. Grey cloak of the Fairy Godparent's Guild. She knew Emory's name before I said it. Knew about the land, about the survey, about my wife, Ilara." His jaw tightened. "She said she could help."

Emory had not looked up from the floor, seeming to be asleep as he stood there.

"And the hatchet," Hollis said.

"She left it. Said it would keep my son safe in the forest."

Neve stood at the workbench while Aldric talked and listened, and his arms rose and fell. *Not daily, but by the minute. There was a bit of fine print that was overlooked,* he thought savagely. Mira was right, every word had been a practiced genie's trick. He'd have to remember to double-check where her magic came from.

"It's the land." He set his hat on his knee. "Forty acres on the eastern edge of our holdings. My wife's family has held it four generations. The Black Forest runs along the boundary, and Sylvaine decided the original survey was wrong. That the land was hers."

Hollis said nothing.

"Ilara didn't accept that." Aldric's hands stilled on the hat brim. "She took the deed and two of our men out to the boundary line to document it properly." He looked at the floor. "She didn't come back."

"The farmhands returned without her," Aldric said. His voice had a flatness of exhaustion. "They said she walked to the boundary marker and vanished."

"And Emory," Mira said. She had come to the edge of the bench without either of them noticing.

"He went after her." Aldric looked at his son. "He had his mother's temper. He was gone before I could get my boots on." He stopped. "He came back. But Sylvaine was at the boundary when he arrived, and she knew who he was, and she told him that Ilara was working in her mines and would continue to do so until the land dispute was settled in her favor."

"And Emory told her what he thought of that," Neve said.

"He told her she was a kidnapper, thief, and a coward. He told her the truth." Aldric's voice was not entirely without a grim kind of pride. "Sylvaine cursed him on the spot. Chop one log a month, she said. It would teach him patience."

"Yes, that's the same woman who commissioned this piece," Mira said.

Neve looked at the floor. At the thin curl of shaving beside the log. His arms rose and fell again, slow and inexorable, and he understood in his shoulder and his wrist and the tightening across his back exactly what the boy had been living for three days. His muscles would only pull harder if he tried to fight it.

"The glass won't chop wood efficiently," he said. "Not the way iron can."

"No." Aldric pressed his hands flat on the counter. "Three days. Tiny progress with each session. He cannot put it down. He carries it when he eats, when he tries to sleep, when he walks the house at night because lying down with it is worse than standing." His voice cracked, and he steadied it. "He is eleven years old."

Emory had sat on the stool Mira pulled forward without being asked. His eyes were closing.

Mira was watching Neve. Not the problem in his hands. Neve.

"Can we melt it down?" she asked Hollis.

"Not yet." Hollis had settled in his chair again, watching everything. "The curse is bound into the glass. We dissolve it now without the right counter potion and we don't know where it goes or what it does when it gets there. Plus, since Neve can't let go of it, I doubt he wants to put his hand in the oven."

Neve stiffened, "Yes, I would like to exhaust more solutions before we resort to that."

"So we wait," Mira said.

"We wait for Mafalda. She is already coming." Hollis looked at Neve. "She said so."

"She said she was coming," Neve agreed. His arms fell. He let them. Fighting every stroke spent him on a battle he could not win over the length of a day. Better to move and save his strength for the fight that would come later.

Mira came and stood beside him. Not reaching for the hatchet again. She stood close enough that he could feel the warmth of her, and she studied his face with a directness that was both assessment and something more than assessment.

"When did you last eat?" she said.

"This morning."

"That was six hours ago." She turned and went to the small cabinet where they kept provisions for long working days.

She came back with bread and hard cheese and set them within reach of him. She poured water from the jug near the furnace. Then she pulled her stool close to the workbench, close enough that her arm was almost against his, and sat as she held out a piece of cheese for him to bite and helped him take a drink of water.

“Eat,” She held out a piece of cheese.

“You’re going to feed me?”

“Do not fuss with me over this. Both your hands are otherwise tied up, and you haven’t eaten.” She knitted her brow at him. “I am serious.” She held the cheese closer.

He opened his mouth and allowed her to feed him, not realizing how hungry he had been.

After he finished, she cleaned up the small plate. She returned to sit next to him, eyeing the hatchet. she opened her sketchbook and picked up her charcoal. She did not say anything else, and the quality of her silence was not absence. Her presence was warm, reassuring.

He had a satisfied feeling that had nothing to do with the cheese. Until his arms rose and fell. The shavings accumulated on the floor in a small pale drift.

"Why would Sylvaine curse a child with an impossible task?"

Emory had fallen asleep on the stool, leaning against the bench, his chin dropping to his chest. His father sat beside him with one hand resting lightly on the boy's shoulder.

"Why don't you two head to the inn across the street?" Hollis said, gathering up some supplies.

"Rest, we'll start fresh in the morning, and when Mafalda from the real Fairy Godparent's Guild arrives, we'll come up with a permanent solution. To reverse this."

Neve hadn't slept. The cursed hatchet had forced him to swing at the wood all night.

The furnace hissed. Outside, the winter morning came in flat and grey.

Mira turned a page in her sketchbook. She had been drawing something he could see from the corner of his eye, cross-sections, angles, lines with measurements beside them. His arm fell. She glanced at the sound of the strike and then returned to her work.

"The directional stabilizer batch," she said eventually. Not looking up. "The starlight potion. It could hold a modification if we can get the hatchet on the bench long enough to work the weave."

"If we can get it on the bench," he said, swinging the hatchet, adding to the little pile of shavings.

"Mafalda might be able to suspend the compulsion to swing. That's different from the binding. Two separate parts of the curse." She made a note in the margin of her sketch. "Long enough for us to work."

"We'll ask her."

She nodded and kept drawing.

Hollis held his tea and said nothing.

Neve's arm fell.

Rose.

Fell.

His shoulder had moved past aching into something with teeth in it. He didn't complain, didn't have the right to. He should never have allowed the hatchet out of the shop. Mira held bread to his mouth, and he ate. She raised the water goblet to his lips, and he drank. At some point, she had shifted on her stool so that her shoulder was against his. He was aware of it with more attention than he had available for it.

Hollis opened his eyes, looked at them both, and said nothing.

"There's a better angle," Mira said. She turned the sketchbook toward him. On the page was a cross-section of the blade, the existing weave in one color and a proposed overlay in another. Clean lines. Angles with measurements. "The secondary weave at ninety degrees to the blade face. It redirects rather than absorbs. Like a lens focusing light. You know, like the case we made for the Beast's rose. All the force goes into the wood at the moment of contact rather than spreading through the blade."

His arm rose and fell. He looked at the drawing.

"That's exactly right," he said. She was so smart and pretty. He remembered lunch. She was also bossy in a way that was good for him.

"I was hoping you would agree," she said. She turned the sketchbook back and kept drawing. "I cross-checked three times with the oldest of our magical glass scrolls."

She had been working on it since Mafalda's letter arrived. Three days of knowing something was wrong with no way to reach the problem. The drawings were all she could do.

The lamp burned low. The furnace hissed. Neve's arm rose and fell through the night, and Mira sat beside him, and Hollis dozed in his chair, and the pale drift of shavings on the floor grew by one small curl at a time.

The bell above the door rang.

Morning light came pale gold through the windows. Mafalda stepped in, her traveling cloak damp at the shoulders. She had come through the night.

Her eyes went to the hatchet in Neve's hands. Then to his face. Then to Mira beside him. Then to the shavings on the floor.

"How long," she said.

"Since yesterday morning," Neve said. His voice was level. His shoulder was not. "But, including the boy, four days."

Mafalda produced her wand. "I can suspend the compulsion to swing. Three days, perhaps four. It won't touch the binding itself. The curse holds and the hatchet stays with you. But you can stop moving."

"Can he set it down?" Mira asked.

"No. The binding holds." Mafalda was already working. "But he can rest while we problem-solve the curse breaking."

She worked for a few minutes. Then she nodded as she put the glass fairy star on the end of her wand and wove in a figure eight around him

"What does the star do?" Mira asked.

"For a fully trained practitioner," Hollis said quietly, "a fairy star is a carrying vessel, for enchantments that cannot survive midnight unanchored. It also magnifies the intent of minor spells. That is why her ceasing spell is holding. In the hands of a giftwright, the intent baked into the glass is the enchantment. The stars can be specifically manufactured for different things."

The compulsion stopped. She put the fairy in her inside pocket with her wand.

Neve's arms stayed at his side. The hatchet was still in his hands, still warm with his own work, but it was simply an object now. A well-made glass hatchet, no longer pulling. He could feel the tension along his shoulders ease.

The silence where the tiny strikes had been was the loudest thing in the workshop as Mafalda leaned over to examine the work.

"Well, I will say one thing: you are definitely no longer an apprentice and much more in line with the master." Mafalda poked the hatchet with her index finger only to have it repelled.

Mira put her hand over his on the handle. Not trying to take it. Just her hand over his, and the warmth of it.

He looked at her hand. Then at her. In his exhaustion, he leaned over and kissed her cheek. "Thanks, Mira."

"Sleep," she said, blushing, but the smile on her lips had washed away the worry. "We'll watch."

“Oh, Mafalda, thank you, too.”

Mafalda laughed. “You're slap-happy, exhausted, boy. Go to bed. We’ll work on it.”

He looked at the sketchbook on the bench. Five pages of calculations. Mafalda was already settling across from Hollis, conjuring tea from somewhere in her sleeves.

“Go up to my quarters, it’ll be quieter than your bed in the office.”

"A few hours," he said.

"As long as you need." Mira walked with him to the stairs, one hand still close to his on the handle, not carrying it for him, just close. "I'll be here when you wake."

He trudged up the stairs. The hatchet went with him.

Mira went back to her stool and opened the sketchbook to turn it toward Mafalda. “This is what my research has shown so far.”

CHAPTER THREE

The Overlay

The first hour was preparation as they combed through all their source material.

Mira cleared the main workbench of everything except the hatchet, the log, the argent twine, and her sketches. She set the lamp at the angle that gave the best light on the blade face and pulled her stool close. Neve sat across from her, the hatchet resting flat between them. Thankfully, it remained still from Mafalda's spell.

"Hold it flat," she said. "Blade face up. I need to see the existing weave before I start the overlay."

He turned his wrist. She bent close with the magnifying lens and traced the argent twine pattern without touching it, her lips moving slightly as she counted angles.

"The diagonal runs steeper than I drew it," she said. "Forty-eight degrees, not forty-five. It changes the overlay calculation." She reached for her charcoal and made a note without looking up. "Give me a moment."

He nodded. Hollis watched from his chair. Mafalda had taken the stool by the window and was reading through the charter document again, a small leather book open beside her for notes. She was muttering language about Sylvaine that Neve was surprised she even knew, let alone used, or anyone in the guild, for that matter.

The workshop was quiet except for the furnace and the soft tap of glass against the workbench edge.

"All right, Mafalda, ready," Mira said. She threaded the first length of thin argent twine onto the finest needle in the workshop and set a small torch on the table to heat it.

She stood and joined them. “Are you sure you want me to lift the enchantment?”

Mira nodded. “All the research I could find on curses suggests that the curse must be active for counteragents to work.”

Neve nodded. “Do it. I am ready.”

Mafalda nodded and waved her wand over the hatchet. Immediately, the compulsion pulled Neve’s arms back and forth to carve out a tiny shaving of the log.

"I start at the heel and work toward the edge. You hold it still as long as you can between strokes. When the compulsion pulls, let it go. Fighting it tires you out, and I need you to be functional tomorrow. So we can melt the hatchet down."

"Understood."

"And don't watch my hands. Watch the door."

He looked up. "Why?"

"Because she felt the modification start on the hatchet she commissioned, and she will come." Mira did not look up from the blade. "Hollis said so this morning while you slept."

Neve looked at Hollis.

"I said it was possible," Hollis said. "I said probable."

"Watch the door," Mira said again.

He looked at the door. At least he had a hatchet if he needed it.

"The work requires attention that leaves no room for anything else," Mafalda explained. "And she will come to try to distract, causing a mistake, causing the curse to trigger and do whatever it was set to do when the hatchet finally broke. But oh! I am ready for her!"

Neve stifled a smile. Fairy godmothers could be vicious when they wanted or needed to be.

Each thread of argent twine had to clear the existing weave without crossing it at the wrong angle. Mira moved in increments so small that an hour's work covered perhaps two inches of blade. She checked the glass for clouding every few minutes, pressing the back of her hand to the flat of the blade, reading the temperature the way a baker reads dough.

"Still clear," she said.

"Good."

She glanced at the sound and returned to work.

By mid-morning, his shoulder was starting to release its dull, persistent ache. Mira reached back without looking and pushed the water cup toward him. Hollis held it up for him, and he drank.

"Thank you," he said.

She did not answer. She was counting threads.

They were perhaps a third of the way through the modification when the bell above the door rang.

Neve did not need to look. He felt Mira go still beside him, one beat, and then her hands resumed their work as if nothing had interrupted them.

Sylvaine stood in the doorway in a forest green cloak. She was smiling. The same smile as the first morning, pleasant and entirely real, worn the way she wore the cloak, as a garment suited to the weather.

“What do we have here?” She said, standing in the doorway. “I have a duly made commission. Where is the boy?”

“Loop hole, Sly...vain,” Mafalda said, straightening up. “Manufacturer’s essence is also in the hatchet. Your victim is resting.”

"Close the door," Neve said. "You're letting the cold in."

She closed it. She moved into the workshop with the same unhurried ease as her first visit, taking in Mafalda at the window, Hollis in his chair, Mira bent over the blade.

"I thought I would find it here," she said. "When I felt the modification beginning, I assumed the father had found you." She looked at the hatchet in Neve's hand, at the new argent twine work along the spine. "Clever. You are redirecting the force."

Neve chopped another sliver off.

"The curse language says split one log," Neve said. "One split. We are making that possible."

She was quiet for a moment. Then she laughed, brief and genuine. "It won't hold. The secondary weave will fight the primary layer. Two or three months, and it degrades." She made a pouty face. “Chop after chop, it will wear down. The hatchet will finally break, and the boy will be my slave.”

"Then we reinforce it again in two or three months," Mira said, looking up at Sylvaine.

“And drive the family into poverty, or drive this shop into poverty?” She made a shrugging gesture. “Same result, only all the land will be mine, not just the disputed land.”

Something moved behind her eyes, quick and assessing. "You understand this changes nothing fundamental. The boy still carries the mine protection of the hatchet. It will get thinner and thinner. Eventually, it breaks." She made a snapping sound with her fingers and a pouty frown.

“No, the boy will not carry it. He’ll never touch this hatchet again, not as long as I can hold it.” Neve chopped another sliver. Wondering what would happen to the boy if the hatchet accidentally broke. Truly, how long could he do this before exhaustion took his own sanity and well-being?

"You built your trap around a glass hatchet that would fail in a year," Mira said, not looking up from the blade. "This one won't."

Sylvaine looked at her. The pleasant smile stayed, but something behind it recalibrated. She had not expected Mira to be the one who understood the timeline.

"You are the cobbler's daughter," Sylvaine said.

"I am a Giftwright," Mira said.

Sylvaine turned back to Neve. "You cannot free the boy. You cannot free the mother. You can delay the inevitable, nothing more. The land dispute remains. The mine remains. I am not unreasonable. I never have been. Forty acres and an acknowledgment of trespass. That is all I have ever wanted. My property back. That's the deal."

"And Ilara Regentry," Neve said.

The room changed. Not in Sylvaine's expression, which did not move, but in the quality of the silence around her.

"She trespassed," Sylvaine said.

"She went to a boundary with a deed," Neve said, chopping a bit of log. "She was documenting a survey line. That is due diligence in a land dispute, and you know it, and the Black Forest charter knows it. All you had to do was present your documents, and if the land was yours, it would have been returned to you. This is nothing but a land grab, and I refuse to help you." He kept his voice even. "Mafalda has been reviewing that charter."

Mafalda did not look up from her document. "The charter requires good faith negotiation before punitive action in land disputes. You skipped that step. Ilara's detention is not protected under the territorial charter. It is unlawful." She turned a page. "I can compel a formal negotiation session. You will attend. The charter binds you whether you hold guild standing or not. But by the last grey hair on my own head, I'll see that you lose it all in a suit regarding the punitive damages you owe the boy and his mother."

Sylvaine was quiet.

"And if I attend," she said, "what exactly are you bringing to the table."

"Something you cannot make yourself," Neve said. "Something you came to this workshop to buy because you knew we were the only shop that could produce it." His arm fell. He let it, one small tap against the workbench edge, and looked at her steadily. "A fairy star built from specific truth and specific love. Something unique. Something that cannot be replicated." He paused. "We are offering you a trade. A proper one. At a table. Through the process the charter requires."

“I am listening.”

“A fairy star! Neve!” Mafalda’s eyes widened.

Sylvaine looked at him for a long moment. The pleasantness stayed in place. But she was thinking.

Neve could feel it the way he could feel heat in metal before it glowed. He had her undivided attention.

"I will attend the negotiation," she said. "I am making no other commitments." She moved toward the door, then paused. "Finish your modification. It is good work, even if it is inconvenient." She looked at Neve directly. "I am sorry for how I used yours, but I need what I need."

She left. The bell chimed.

Nobody spoke for a moment.

"She meant that," Mira said. She had not looked up from the blade.

"Yes," Neve said. "It doesn't change what she did."

“It also doesn’t change that she’s an evil git!” Mafalda said.

"No," Mira said. "But it changes what she might do next." She set the needle down and straightened her back. "I need the starlight potion. The small batch."

“A fairy star? Neve. That is the highest magical treasure.” Mafalda said, with a pleading look.

“I know. Don’t forget who my brother is, who trained me before Hollis did. And not one grey hair on your head has to be sacrificed." He smiled as he chopped another sliver off.

Neve used his foot to scoot the bucket over. "Hollis and I can talk Mira through it. She's good at what she does, and female. That'll make a difference." He smiled. "And you know it."

CHAPTER FOUR

The Star

The deed rested in the middle of the workbench, unfolded, the paper heavy with age and bearing signs of repeated handling and examination. Aldric had pressed it flat with both hands and then stepped back from it, as if stepping back was the only respect he could still show for his wife's handwriting.

Emory stood at the window. He had slept and eaten twice, and the hollowness around his eyes had lessened enough that he looked eleven again rather than eighty. He did not focus on the deed. Instead, he watched the hatchet in Neve's hands as he motioned for Aldric to prepare equipment for Mira, who was mixing the potion for the glass star.

Aldric set the small crucible on the stand above the lamp and looked at Mira across the bench.

"You're making it," he said. “You’re going to give her treasure?”

Neve nodded. “It’ll close the issue and keep your entire family safe from her once and for all.”

Mira looked up at Neve. "You're the more experienced glassworker."

"I am also holding a hatchet. A cursed one." He adjusted his grip, both hands, the weight of it settled across his palms. "But that is not the reason. You have the right instincts for this kind of work. The mining boots. The modification weave. You understand how something takes force and redirects it rather than absorbing it until it breaks." He nodded toward the crucible. "A fairy star is the same principle. You are not making glass that only holds truth. You are making glass that carries it somewhere useful. Fairy glass, if you remember, is also how Mafalda carried the glass slippers to Cinderella."

Mira looked at the deed. Then at the crucible. Then at him.

"Tell me how to start," she said.

"The paper first. It goes in whole. Don't tear it. Then the red potion on top of it."

She picked up the deed with both hands. She looked at Aldric. "You do have another copy, right?"

He nodded once. "To free my son and my wife, it is of no consequence. But yes, there is a master copy with the king's scribe."

She set it into the crucible. The lamp was already burning high, and the paper caught at the edges almost immediately, the ink darkening before it disappeared, becoming burned at the edges as she poured the small bottle of red potion on it.

"Don't look away from it," Neve said. "Watch the whole thing go. Every word. You are witnessing it, not just burning it. That matters."

She nodded. "Right, intention matters." She watched. The survey notes Ilara had written in the margins went last, the smaller handwriting holding a moment longer than the print before the paper curled entirely to ash.

"Now roll the gather," Neve said. "Small. The star is not a large object. It needs to be the size of something a fairy godmother would actually use, and stay on the end of her wand."

Mira took the blowpipe and gathered the potion-treated argent twine from the pot he had prepared before the deed went in. Small and precise. She brought it to the bench and set the gather at the marver.

"Work it into the ash while it's still soft," Neve said. "Fold the ash in, don't stir it. Folding preserves the structure. Stirring just mixes."

"Like pastry," she said, and folded with the long, metal pinchers, keeping safely away from the still molten glass.

"Yes." He had not thought of it that way, but it was exactly right. "Exactly like pastry."

Hollis made a small sound from his chair that was not quite a laugh. “Some of us didn’t have a chef to prepare our meals.”

Neve shrugged as the hatchet swung, shaving off a little bit of wood

The glass took the ash in slowly, the gather going grey and then settling into something that was not quite clear and not quite clouded, a clarity of depth that ordinary magical glass did not have. Mira worked without asking questions. When she reached a point she was unsure of, she paused and looked at him, and he told her what to do next, and she did it. No argument, no second-guessing. She trusted his instruction the way he had trusted Hollis' teaching when he had started.

Hollis watched from his chair near the office.

"There, pinch it, into the star shape." Neve pointed with the hatchet.

"What does it do," Emory said, from the window ledge he'd sat on. Not a question precisely. More as if he was working something out as he watched Mira use the long pinchers to form the star in the soft glass.

"It carries something of your mother's into the negotiation. It also has your family's original intention to purchase the lands, and which lands they were specifically," Neve said, not telling the entire truth. This star, while true fairy glass, would not be like Mafalda's. It would function more like a hybrid of truth glass and fairy glass. "It carries her intent. Her certainty that she was right. Everything she brought to that boundary line with her."

Emory looked at the gather in Mira's hands. "And Sylvaine will want it."

"She will want it very much," Neve said. "She cannot make one herself. She knows what went into it, and she knows she cannot replicate it. Only a very skilled giftwright can make this. And, to make it stronger for the intention here, only a woman can make it. That is the negotiation. Fairy stars require difficult fire-based potions before the glass can even be made."

“A woman?” Emory walked over, eyes fixed on Mira as she worked.

“Be careful, sweetheart, this can still burn you. It’s still hot enough to melt the argent twine.” She rolled the tube, applying pressure with the pinchers to continue to form the star's points.

“Exactly,” Neve said, smiling. “Mira isn’t a mother, but carries the mother’s concern, as does the document. You will see soon.” And if all went as planned, Sylvaine would regret this.

If he made it, it would be more like Mafalda’s.

Emory was quiet for a moment. Then he said, "How do you know it works?"

Mira's hands slowed fractionally. Then resumed.

Neve looked at the boy. "We give it a neutral test without activating it."

"How."

"Someone touches it who is not its maker, but also not a full magical person. Usually, another magical trade person. The glass responds to genuine contact. It either lights from inside or it doesn't." He shifted his weight. Both hands on the hatchet. The overlay was working. The chopping had slowed to just three or four every half hour or so. "The test requires my hands free."

Silence. Both Aldric and Emory shook their heads. Emory stopped as a pained expression crossed his face.

“I can....” Emory started to say.

Aldric said, "No."

Emory had already straightened. "I'll take it back."

"No," Aldric said again, more firmly. "Emory, you have slept two nights without it. You are not picking it up again."

“No,” Neve agreed. “Children aren’t allowed to handle cursed hatchets. Not under any circumstances.”

“What about him? He’s a giftwright. Can’t he test it?” Aldric pointed to Hollis.

“Once upon a time, yes, but I am very ill. My fading energy isn’t strong enough to test it. We’d need another giftwright. I’m about as useful as a total non-magic.”

"Oh, that will take time! It's one hour," Emory said. He was looking at Neve, not his father. "How long does the test take?"

"The test itself is a moment," Neve said. "But if it needs adjustment, longer. Certainly, less than an hour." He kept his voice level.

"Then I'll hold it for one hour. Father, you can time it." Emory's jaw had set. He appeared to be only explaining himself out of courtesy. "You need your hands. The star needs testing. My mother is still in the mine." He looked at his father. "It is not only me that needs saving."

Aldric opened his mouth.

Closed it, nodded. “One hour.”

"Well, it'll take time to cool down long enough to worry about it. Right now, it'll be hot enough to still melt some forms of metal. There is time."

The workshop was quiet except for the furnace and the soft sound of Mira working the gather.

"Come back this evening." Neve said, chopping another shaving off the log. "I should be able to test it then. It just needs a touch."

Neve looked at the boy, chin set, making a case as cleanly as any guild negotiator. He was not wrong. It would be faster for the boy to hold it, and the hatchet had been tempered from its original intensity. The star could not go to Sylvaine untested. That was a disaster waiting to happen.

On the other hand, Mafalda could not test it because a fairy godmother's touch on a glass star would imprint the magic as hers, and the star would carry Mafalda's intent rather than Ilara's intent to be free of Sylvaine. Neve could not test it while his hands were occupied. Mira could not test it because she had made it, and a maker testing their own work was not a test at all.

Hollis shook his head slowly. "My hands are not the right hands for this anymore." He said it without elaboration. Neve understood. A dying man's touch on a star built from a living woman's truth and love, constructed by a maker who might one day be a good and protective mother, was simply not strong enough to test it.

It needed the male energy of a someday protective father, not someone who never wanted to be a father. Unless...

“You wouldn’t happen to have any latent magic?” Neve asked Aldric. “You are a father, you could test it, even with latent, untrained magic.”

Aldric shook his head. “Not one drop of magical blood. Can’t even brew a cold and flu potion.”

“Father! I can hold it for an hour, for Mother. I can do it. Neither of you raised a son who wouldn’t help you in your moment of need.”

“Alright. Alright, one hour.”

Aldric nodded, “Let’s leave them to work and go eat. You’re sure this will work?”

“I am never sure of anything,” Neve shook his head, thinking this boy would make an excellent duke one day. “But I believe this is the best chance we have of getting her to give the cursed hatchet to me to dispose of and freeing your wife.”

Later in the evening, Aldric and Emory returned.

"One hour," Neve said. To Emory. Not to Aldric. "You hand it back to me the moment the hour is up, whether the test is complete or not. Agreed."

Emory nodded.

"Say it."

"I agree," Emory said. "One hour. I give it back when you say."

Neve held out the hatchet.

Emory took it in both hands. His face went tight for a moment, the old compulsion settling back into his shoulders, and then he breathed out and steadied. He crossed to the wall and stood with his back against it, the log on the floor in front of him, and his arm began to fall.

Neve turned to Mira.

"Finishing steps," he said. "Then we find out."

The star sat on the iron cooling square at the center of the bench, now cooled to the room's temperature. It was small, the size of a large coin, with five uneven points, but perfect at the same time. The ash from the deed ran through it in faint gray threads, visible only when the light caught it at the right angle.

Mira stepped back from it. She looked at it once, checking finished work, then set down her tools. Neve couldn't tell if the look was pride at the work or surprise that she did it.

"Excellent work, Mira. I couldn't have taught it better myself." Hollis leaned over to look at the star.

Across the workshop, Emory's arm fell. Rose. Fell. The shavings had been accumulating again for the better part of an hour, a small pale drift against the baseboard. He had not complained except to say it was good that it didn't swing every minute on the minute. He had not looked at the clock. He stood with his back to the wall as agreed, and when his arm fell, he let it fall, and he watched the workshop with dark eyes that missed very little.

Neve reached across and touched the star with two fingers.

The light came from inside it, not reflected, not borrowed from the lamp above the bench. It was the quality of light that truth glass produced when it recognized genuine contact, steady, clear, and without any performance. The gray threads caught the light like flecks of quartz, and in that moment, the threads resolved into something almost legible.

Using a magnifying glass, one thing became clear: the ghost of Ilara's handwriting, the survey margin notes she had made on the day she walked to the boundary line and did not come back. Additionally, the notes from the scribe marked the property lines and usage rights, including passage of the king's forces, merchants to the mines, and peasants to the river.

Then it steadied. The light remained, low and constant, the way a good fire held its heat.

Mira let out a breath. Just the one.

"It's right," Neve said.

"I know," she said. "I could feel it when the ash went in and again when I blew the intention into it."

Neve smiled, just before Mira had warned Emory to be safe around the glass. The intent to protect a child. He wasn't sure what effect that would have on the truth glass, but it had to be a good one.

Hollis said nothing from his chair. His expression said everything it needed to.

Neve moved his right hand back to the handle. He looked at Emory.

"Your hour is done," he said, wiggling his fingers for the hatchet. "The fairy star is perfect."

Emory crossed the workshop without being asked and held the hatchet out in both hands. Neve took it. His fingers clasped tight around the handle, and the compulsion settled back into his shoulders, but thankfully, didn't force a chop, yet.

"Well?" Emory said.

"It's ready." Neve nodded toward the star on the velvet square. "Tomorrow morning, we take it to the guild."

Emory looked at the star for a long moment. Then he looked at Neve.

"She'll come," he said. "If you call her to the guild."

"She'll come," Neve agreed. He pointed to the star. "She wants what's on that square. And the guild charter will do the rest."

Emory nodded once, the same gesture his father used, the family resemblance landing cleanly. Then he went to find Aldric.

Mira picked up the star with both hands and wrapped it in the velvet. She did not look at Neve while she worked, but when she set it aside, she said, without preamble, "You should sleep."

"I know."

"I mean, tonight. Actual sleep."

"I'll get half an hour at a time. Unless Mafalda comes back." He shifted the hatchet's weight. Both hands, the settled familiar pull of it. "I can sleep, though. The overlay really suppressed it. It's not causing muscle spasms anymore."

She looked at him. The lamp light was low, the workshop quiet around them, Hollis already dozing in his chair with his tea gone cold.

"Then go," she said. "I'll lock up."

He went to his cot in the side office, carrying the chopping log.

Chapter Five

The Guild

The Fairy Godparents Guild occupied a building on the north end of the high street, three stories of dressed stone with a blue door that had been the same shade of blue for longer than anyone in Silverneve could reliably remember. The crossed wands seal announcing "Protecting the Realm" stood out prominently against its hot pink background.

Mafalda had sent word the previous evening. The guild clerk had confirmed by return paper bird before the workshop lamp burned out.

Sylvaine would attend. She had not sent a reply herself. The clerk noted she had read the summons and nodded.

They arrived at the ninth hour. Neve carried the hatchet in both hands and the log under one arm, which drew looks on the high street that he did not have the energy to address. Mira walked beside him with the velvet-wrapped star in her coat pocket, one hand resting over it. Emory walked behind them with his father, and Hollis came last, moving at his own pace with his good coat on and his breathing careful in the cold morning air.

Neve had told him to stay at the workshop.

Hollis had looked at him with the expression he reserved for suggestions he found beneath comment and put his coat on.

The guild chamber was on the ground floor, a long room with a table down the center and chairs on both sides and guild seals worked into the plaster above the windows. A clerk sat at a smaller desk near the door with a ledger open and an inkwell freshly filled. Two guild witnesses occupied chairs at the far end of the table, neither of them people Neve recognized.

His brother, Duke of Silverneve, Garrett sat behind the table with the village scribe next to him. He gave Neve a reassuring nod as his eyes found the glass hatchet. Aldric and Emory sat on the other side of Garrett in their best noble court robes.

Neve nodded back. Whatever happened here today would be enforced at the highest levels.

Sylvaine was already there, wearing a steel blue cloak that suspiciously resembled the light grey of the guild. She sat on the left side of the table, hands folded on the table surface. She looked as she always looked, unhurried, pleasant, entirely at home in a room that was not hers. Her eyes went to the hatchet first, then to Neve's face, then to Mira's coat pocket.

She knew what was in it. Neve could see that she knew.

Mafalda took the chair directly across from Sylvaine. She set her leather document case on the table and opened it without looking at anyone. Aldric moved to sit beside Mafalda. Emory joined his father and looked at the table.

Neve set the log on the floor beside his chair and sat with the hatchet across his knees, both hands on the handle. Mira sat next to him. Hollis took the chair at the near end of the table and said nothing, breathing slowly and deliberately as the doctor had told him.

The clerk looked at Mafalda. "All parties present. You may proceed."

Mafalda set three documents on the table. "For the record. The territorial charter of the Black Forest boundary, section twelve: good-faith negotiation requirements. The guild expulsion record for Sylvaine, formerly of the eastern district, fourteen months prior. And a draft binding contract covering the terms of this negotiation." She looked up at Sylvaine. "All three are already entered into the guild ledger. Copies will be held here regardless of today's outcome."

Sylvaine looked at the documents. "You've been busy."

"I've been thorough," Mafalda said. "There is a difference."

"And the star," Sylvaine said. Her eyes moved to Mira's coat pocket again. "I was told there would be a star."

"There is," Neve said. "After the terms are agreed and the contract is signed. Not before."

Sylvaine considered that. "What are the terms?"

Mafalda folded her hands. "Ilara Regentry is released from the mine today, within the hour, and returned to her family unharmed. The curse on the hatchet is dissolved and the object surrendered to the Giftwright Workshop for disposal. The land dispute goes to independent guild assessment within thirty days, with both parties bound to accept the assessor's finding on the boundary line. You will make no further punitive or magical contact with the Regentry family, their lands, their household, or their associates." She paused. "In exchange, you receive the fairy star."

Sylvaine was quiet for a moment. "The assessment may not find in my favor."

"Correct," Mafalda said. "It may not. It's a risk. Unfortunately, we do not have jurisdiction there. However, the Duke of Silverneve is here and has sworn to hear the complaint as a neutral party at a later date."

"Then I may surrender the mine access and have only the star."

"You come away with a legal resolution and your name on a binding guild contract rather than a second expulsion hearing for unlawful detention. One that would result in incarceration," Mafalda's voice did not change. "And for heaven's sake, an expertly made fairy star is more than fifty thousand gold crowns. You know full well that's the reason not every fairy godparent has one. Do you have fifty thousand gold crowns to purchase it properly?"

Sylvaine looked at the table. At her own folded hands. At the guild seals above the windows. "That would be my entire life savings."

"Then let's stop pretending that surrendering any land you own, or think you own, is walking away with nothing," Mafalda said, seeming to try to keep her voice even. "When a free, expertly made fairy star is in play."

Emory said, "She's stalling."

Aldric put a hand on his arm.

"I'm not stalling." Sylvaine looked at the boy directly for the first time since she had come into the room. "I'm deciding. After all, the curse will trigger, and you will be my slave, alongside your dear mother. That is two birds in my hand versus the larger more succulent birds in the bush."

"You decided before you walked in," Aldric said. He was not rude about it, just precise. "You came because you want the star. You had to know what the terms would be roughly, because Fairy Godmother Mafalda isn't subtle about the charter, and you've read the charter. You're deciding whether you can negotiate any of the terms, and you're deciding that you can't, because the clause about the assessment is the only term that costs you anything, and if the land were actually yours, the assessment would say so. However, we both know, it won't. The land is mine, and I am a victim here, too. My son will trade for his mother; I will trade for my son, but perhaps I won't trade for me. What about Giftwright Neve? Perhaps he won't bend the knee to your demands and demand justice for what you did to him?"

Mafalda smiled, "It's true, there is more here at play than just the boy, his mother, and the land. There is the matter of the fraudulent commissioning of the hatchet and possessing the dangerous potion-infused supplies to make it. That's not even on the table for negotiation."

The room was quiet.

“I heard you took the hatchet yesterday to free the Giftwright to finish the star,” Sylvaine looked at the boy for a long moment. "You have your mother's mind."

"Yes," Emory said. "She's in your mine. My family has me, and I have them. I took the hatchet and would take it again, even longer if it meant freeing her."

Something crossed Sylvaine's face, quick and unguarded, there and gone before it could be named.

"The star," she said to Neve. "Let me see it."

Neve looked at Mira, barely able to keep a straight face. Sylviane thought he did it. Thought the opposite male energy had been used to make it.

Mira reached into her coat pocket and set the velvet square on the table. She unwrapped it with both hands and left it sitting in the square of cloth, five uneven points, the grey threads of ash just visible in the guild room light.

Sylvaine did not touch it. She looked at it the way she had looked at Mira's weave work in the workshop on the first morning, with admiration, as if she were gazing upon a great diamond.

"You made this," she said to Mira.

"Yes," Mira said, glancing at Neve. "Under the supervision of Neve. Due to his hands being bound to the hatchet handle, but your information is correct, Neve finished the process."

"How old are you?"

"I am sorry, I don't see how my age is relevant."

"Agreed," Mafalda said. "It's not. It's a certified fairy star. End of story. I'll file the certificate myself."

Sylvaine looked at the star for another moment. Then she picked up Mafalda's pen and signed the contract with a clean, unhesitating signature. She set the pen down and looked at the clerk. "Open the mine access at the eastern boundary. Now, please. The woman inside is free to go."

The clerk made a note and sent a paper bird through the window without being asked.

Mafalda countersigned. The guild seal appeared at the bottom of the contract, shimmered, and held.

The curse released without ceremony. One moment, the hatchet had weight. The density of something with malice behind it. The next moment it didn't. Neve sat very still. His shoulder ached. His wrists ached. He had not noticed, until that second, how much they had been aching all along.

He set it on the table.

Aldric put both arms around his son and said nothing at all.

Mafalda slid the velvet with the star across the table to Sylvaine. Sylvaine picked it up with both hands. She held it up, and the guild room light came through it, the grey threads brightening, and Ilara's handwriting appeared again, the survey notes from the boundary line, steady and clear.

She looked at it for a long time, a puzzled look on her face.

"It's beautiful," she said, finally.

"Yes," Neve said. "It is."

Sylvaine wrapped the star in her handkerchief and stood. She took her cloak from the chair back and pulled it on. At the door, she stopped and looked back at Mira.

"Come and find me," she said, "when you've made three more."

The star flared once, bright enough to leave an afterimage, and Sylvaine was gone. Her cloak settled to the floor in an empty heap. Only the star lay on top of the cloak.

“Well,” Mafalda walked over and picked up the sparkling star. “She didn’t do her research on fairy stars.”

Mira smiled at Neve as he stood. “But Neve did. When she cannot abuse, the star will let her go.”

She pointed at Neve. "You, on the other hand, knew exactly what you were giving her," Mafalda said. It wasn't quite a question.

Neve smiled. "My brother Corvin. The only one of my seven brothers born with full magic. He used a fairy star once to bring in a dangerous fugitive. Three warrants hadn't been served on the man, well, goblin. The star made it possible."

Mafalda looked at him for a moment. "And you gave one to Sylvaine."

"I gave her one built by a giftwright, using protective feminine magic," Neve said. "There is a difference. Yours was made by a male for the purpose of holding and enhancing things. You couldn't put a person in there. The palace had commissioned that for the king's guard to bring in a dangerous goblin known for tricking new mothers out of their newborns. Corvin used it to imprison him, with the magical intent that he learn ethics before he could let himself out. He's still imprisoned."

"Rumpelstiltskin. I remember him." Mafalda smirked, stuffing the star into her robes. "May that be a very long time for both Sylvaine and Skin."

"What just happened?" Emory asked, looking at the cloak on the floor.

"Your mother's words and intention to protect your future. And Mira's good and kind heart in trying to protect you from the molten glass." Neve smiled, twirling the hatchet with one hand. "You see, fairy stars must have equal and opposite male and female energy to do the bidding of the fairy. To have a double male or a double female puts the fairy at risk of the intention in the truth glass. If I had made it, it wouldn't have imprisoned her. It would have only stopped the abuse of people. However, she could buy a new wand and continue. This way, she'll actually have to change to get out."

"That is amazing!" Emory said. "Whoever said giftwrights are half-mages doesn't know how magic works at all."

"Agreed," Hollis said, standing to stand by Neve's side.

"So, Mother can come home?"

"Yes," Mafalda said. "We'll send someone to make sure the notice was enforced this evening.

Mafalda gathered her documents. Hollis sat at the end of the table with his hands folded and his eyes closed, breathing carefully, his good coat still buttoned to the throat. Aldric was still holding Emory, one hand on the back of the boy's head. Emory had his face turned into his father's shoulder, and his shoulders were moving, and he was not making any sound at all.

Neve left the hatchet on the table and looked at Mira.

She was looking at the cloak on the floor.

"Three more," she said quietly. "Why would she want that? She just admitted she couldn't buy one, let alone three."

"I don't know. It can't mean anything good, though," Neve said.

Mira picked up her tools from beside her chair and put them in her coat pocket. She looked at the table, at the hatchet lying harmless on the wood, at the pale velvet cloth that had held the star, at the guild seals in the plaster.

"We should get Hollis home," she said. "The cold is bad for him."

"Yes," Neve said.

He picked up the hatchet. It was just glass now, well-made glass with argent twine through the spine and his mark on the handle, and nothing else. He carried it out into the winter morning, and Mira walked beside him, and behind them Hollis came slowly with Aldric's hand under his elbow, and the high street went about its business around all of them.

Chapter Six

The Estate

The road east ran through bare winter fields and then into a stretch of beech wood where the light came through the branches in flat grey sheets. The Regentry's noble carriage, pulled by six horses, swayed with the road.

Mira smiled. "Since becoming a giftwright, I have ridden in fine carriages more than in my entire life as a cobbler."

"It's our honor to have you," Emory said, then, turning his attention to Neve, asked. "I'll bet you have, though. Father says you're the Duke of Silvern-eve's brother."

"I am, and I have." Neve nodded, smiling, but in his heart felt that Aldric was more forgiving of Neve's oversight that kicked this whole unfortunate adventure off than he would have been.

Aldric seemed to be thinking along the same lines. "I did worry about you. But once you came up with that twist of contract with the fairy star, I knew it had been a genuine error."

"My apologies. I sent word to the guild, just didn't get it back in time." He looked out the window. He'd have to commission a magical contract that had a no-harm clause in it.

"So, the hatchet is just a big piece of glass?" Emory asked.

"Yes, well, normal truth glass, because of the treated argent twine in it. But otherwise, no longer special," Neve explained.

The hatchet rode in Neve's coat pocket. He kept his hand near it out of habit.

"She'll be there before us," Aldric said. He had said it twice already. Each time it sounded less like a statement and more like something he was testing to see if it would hold. “Three birds confirming she was home, resting, and recovering. The last bird was from her.”

"The guild's messenger paper bird is faster than horses," Neve said. "She was probably out within the hour. What kind of mines did Sylvaine have?"

“Argent,” Emory said, digging in his pocket for a piece of dried beef.

“Argent? You mean silver,” Mira said, looking at Neve with a sense of dread crossing her face.

“So, our argent twine?” Neve said, closing his eyes, blood silver. And he’d been part of the demand that created the supply.

“I suppose so.” Aldric nodded and looked at the road.

“Yes, in particular, magical silver,” Aldric laughed. “Funnily enough, she supplies more than half of the argent twine used in magical potions. When she said she didn’t have the money for the fairy star, I was left wondering what in the name of the realm she spends her money on.”

Neve was pulled out of his supply chain thought. What did she spend her money on? She should have been able to easily afford a fairy star...even the three extra ones she teased. Giftwrights weren't the only ones who used argent twine. She'd also asked for Mira, once she completed three fairy stars, not him.

Hollis had only made two in this entire sixty-year career.

Neve now regretted they could question her inside the star. The only way out for her to truly change. The magical intent of the maternal protection was absolute, and unyielding, no different than a mother would absolutely keep her child from danger.

"What will they do with her mines and land?" Emory asked.

Aldric shrugged. "That's up to the king's land council. I'll just be glad to have those forty acres settled finally."

He'd have to send a paper bird to Garrett. That mine needed an audit, now. How many missing people or con victims would be there or wait around to be recorded as victims? They needed to know the full extent of Sylvaine's crimes.

The estate came into view as the beech wood thinned, a stone manor of moderate size set back from a low wall, bare rose canes along the south face, and smoke from two chimneys. Practical and well-kept, the house of people who used what they had and maintained it carefully.

A woman stood in the open gate.

She was perhaps thirty-five, dark-haired, road dust still on her clothes, still moving even now that she had stopped, the way a person does when they have been going too long to simply stand still. She was thinner than she should have been. Her hands, when Aldric reached her, were rough from mine work.

Emory jumped out of the carriage before it had fully stopped.

"Mother!"

He crossed the yard at a run, and she caught him with both arms, and neither of them said anything for a long moment. She had her face pressed into the top of his head and her eyes closed, and Emory had both fists in the back of her coat, and the yard was quiet except for the horses and the rooks in the bare elms at the wall.

Aldric reached them and put his arms around both of them.

“You’d have been proud, the way he stood up to her.” Aldric hugged both of them.

Neve looked away. Mira was already looking at the rose canes along the wall, giving the family the only privacy the open yard allowed.

After a while, Ilara looked up. Her eyes found Neve across the yard.

"You're the Giftwright," she said.

"Yes."

She studied him for a moment. "You held the hatchet, so my son didn’t have to."

"I did. It was the minimum I could do. I had no idea she was going to do that."

She nodded, the same decisive nod as Aldric and Emory, two generations of the same gesture.

“You also knew about the manufacturer loophole? So you aren’t entirely without education.” She eyed him, still not taking her hands off Emory. “A journeyman just happens to know contracts and loopholes?”

“I came to my apprenticeship with a noble education. My father was the former Duke of Silverneve. It’s true. And of course, once I realized what happened, what she tricked me into doing, I immediately started to find loopholes."

She nodded again, her expression softening, "I went to school with Garrett. Pratt, but I suppose we all were at that age. Come inside. Both of you. You look like you haven't slept in a week."

"Four days," Neve smiled. "Yes, he can be. But at least he's fair."

"He was, Mother," Emory said, looking at her. "He lent his office's magical scribe to record the contract so the guild would have full enforcement powers."

The meal was simple and substantial, roast meat and root vegetables, and bread still warm from the oven. A fire in the hall. Candles on the table. Emory ate steadily and, between bites, told his mother everything: the workshop, the shavings on the floor, the star, the guild chamber, Sylvaine, and the cloak on the floor.

"The mine," Neve said, when the meal had been going long enough that the worst of the tension had settled. "What were they pulling out when you were there?"

Ilara looked at him over her cup. "Argent. Magical grade for potion blending and twine making. They had me on the sorting line, not the face."

"Sorting line," Neve said. "So you saw the full yield."

"Ilara, you don't have to talk about it if you don't want to." Aldric glanced between Neve and his wife, who waved him off.

"Everything that came out of the face came through sorting first." She set her cup down. "Why?"

"The argent twine used in this workshop comes from a supplier in the eastern district." He kept his voice even. "I don't know yet if it's the same mine."

Ilara was quiet for a moment. Then she looked at her hands, the roughness across her palms from the sorting work.

"She had eight workers on the face when I arrived," she said slowly. "By the time I left there were eleven. Three new ones in the time I was there." She looked up. "I assumed they were taken like I was. I didn't ask. I do know at least two of them had been hired."

"Let's talk about something more interesting," Aldric said, finishing off his wine.

"This is interesting," Ilara said. "And I am in a position to give testimony that can help someone. We can have our mage send a bird to the Duke of Silverneve through Neve. We can get some real help. He's the queen's nephew."

"Well, strictly speaking, I am also the queen's nephew, but I would be very happy to send a message to Garrett for you using my familial channels."

Ilara sat back in her chair. Her eyes moved to Emory, then to Aldric, then back to Neve. The sharpness that had been in her face since the gate was reorganizing itself into something more focused.

"Wait, did you say some appeared to be hired?" Emory asked. "Who would willingly work for her? How did you know they were hired, Mother?"

"Their attitude was different from the workers like... like... from the workers like me, who were forced there. The foreman kept a ledger," she said. "Locked box, top shelf of the tool room. He was careful about it. Too careful for a simple production record."

"A locked ledger in a magical silver mine," Neve said. “I wonder what she was really up to?”

"With workers who appeared without notice and no visible means of having traveled there, but as I said, their attitude was not that of someone kidnapped and forced into labor. They seemed relieved to be there." Ilara's voice had gone flat and precise. "I thought I was the only one compelled. I assumed the others were there by choice because they moved freely, and I did not. Well, four others and I." She stopped. "But I was on a sorting line with a cursed tool. They were on a face with iron picks. They wouldn't have needed cursed tools if they were willing."

The table was quiet.

Emory had set down his fork.

"The yield," Neve said. "Was it consistent? Or were they pushing harder recently?"

Ilara thought about it. "Harder. The foreman was pressing the face crew for longer hours the last two weeks. He said the vein was narrowing." She looked at Neve directly. "You think the vein runs onto our land."

"I think it's worth finding out," Neve said. "And I think the ledger in that tool room is worth finding before anyone else does."

Ilara looked at Aldric. Something passed between them, the shorthand of people who had been making decisions together for a long time.

"The mine is half a mile from the eastern boundary," she said. "I know the layout." She folded her hands on the table. "I can take you there in the morning." She turned to Emory. “Tell me again about your bravery.”

Ilara listened without interrupting. When Emory finished, she was quiet for a moment.

"You held the hatchet again," she said. "Voluntarily."

"For an hour," Emory said. "So Neve could test the star. You were still in the mine. We needed him, not me. Father tried to stop me, but I wouldn’t have it. Even Master Neve tried to stop me, but I wouldn’t have that either. Not until you were home."

“Thank you, my darling.” Ilara looked at him for a long moment. Then she looked at Neve. “What becomes of the cursed thing now?”

"The overlay," Neve said. "Now that the curse is dissolved, we should remove it cleanly. The modification was built to manage the curse. Without the curse, it has nothing to work against, and modified glass that has no purpose gets brittle." He set the hatchet on the table. "Emory should do it. One clean chop. That's all it will take."

Emory looked at the hatchet. "And then?"

"It breaks," Neve said. "That's what it's supposed to do."

They went out to the woodpile behind the kitchen. Aldric set a log on the block. The night was cold and clear, a hard frost coming, the stars very bright above the bare elms.

Neve removed the overlay with two passes of his thumb along the spine, feeling the modification release cleanly, the glass going from reinforced to simply glass beneath his hands. He set the hatchet on the block.

Emory picked it up in both hands. He stood for a moment, feeling the weight of it, his face unreadable.

Then he brought it down.

The chop was clean and honest, a boy's strength and nothing else, and the last vestiges of magic in the log split neatly down the center. The hatchet struck through and hit the block beneath, and the glass shattered on contact, five or six large pieces and a scatter of smaller ones catching the starlight as they fell.

Emory stepped back, a satisfied smile on his face. “That’s what was supposed to happen, wasn’t it. I was to be impatient like a little boy and do this. That would have made me a slave?”

Neve nodded. “She’s truly an evil woman. That’s in the core of who she is. She won’t be escaping that star anytime soon.”

The pieces lay on the block and in the surrounding snow, bright and still.

Neve crouched and gathered them before they could dissolve, fitting the larger shards into his coat pocket the way he always handled broken glass, quickly and without cutting himself. One small piece had already gone, melting into the snow without a mark. He got the rest.

Nobody asked him why.

He stood. Emory was looking at the split log, both halves fallen to either side of the block, clean cut.

"I did that," Emory said.

"You did," Neve said.

Emory picked up one half of the log and carried it toward the kitchen door. After a moment, Aldric picked up the other half and followed him.

“I think this log would produce the best heat for the evening,” Emory said, smiling.

The guest rooms were on the upper floor, two doors across a narrow corridor. Mira's was the larger one, Neve's had a better view of the frost-silvered garden below.

He was standing at the window when he heard her door open.

She appeared in the corridor in her coat, which meant she had not intended to sleep either.

"Garden?" she said.

"Yes," he said.

The garden was small and formal, laid out in quadrants with stone paths between them, everything cut back for winter. A bench sat at the center where the paths crossed. They sat on it without discussion. Their breath came in small clouds in the cold air.

The house was quiet around them. Somewhere inside, a door opened and closed, Aldric and Ilara's voices briefly audible and then not. In the stables, a horse shifted.

"She'll recover," Mira said. "Ilara. The mine work was hard but she's strong."

"Yes," Neve said.

Mira looked at the frost on the cut-back rose canes along the wall. "Sylvaine wanted three more stars."

"I know."

"I've been thinking about why."

"So have I." He turned the coat pocket where the shards were. "She's imprisoned in the star. She can't commission anything herself."

"Someone else could commission them on her behalf." Mira's voice was careful and precise, the same tone she used when she was working out load-bearing angles. "If she told someone, before the guild chamber, what to ask for."

Neve looked at her.

"The three more stars," he said quietly, shaking his head.

Mira waited.

"A fairy star carries an unlimited quantity of anything." He kept his voice low. "Tainted argent past any inspection point. But also people." He paused. "Drop someone hundreds of miles from home with nothing. No landmarks. No money. No contacts. No language, if she went far enough. You don't need locks. The mine doesn't need walls if the world outside it is incomprehensible; you stay where there is food and shelter."

Mira said nothing.

"Ilara's workers. The ones who arrived without road dust or gear or any account of how they got there. The ones who seemed relieved." He looked at the frost on the rose canes. "That's what that was. They weren't relieved. They were defeated."

"Three stars," Mira said. "Three supply lines."

"Rotating. She could have built something that fed itself indefinitely. Hundreds of miles between the victims and anyone who might recognize them or help them. No danger on the road of them being freed. A clean supply of labor with nowhere to run to."

The garden was very quiet.

"You didn't tell Aldric," Mira said.

"They've had enough for one night."

She nodded once and did not push it. After a moment, she said, "Garrett needs that ledger. Not eventually."

"I sent the bird before dinner."

She looked at him.

"I wasn't sure why yet," he said. "I just knew."

The quiet came back. Her shoulder stayed against his. Neither of them went inside for a long while.

"It's a concern for another day," she said. "Not tonight. And we'd certainly never take a commission for three fairy stars at the same time."

"No, you're right." he agreed. "Not tonight. Tonight, we can be thankful that not just anyone can make them."

The frost was settling more heavily on the garden. The stars were very clear. Mira's shoulder was against his. The warmth of her steady and familiar.

He turned toward her. She was already looking at him, close enough that he could see the frost had caught in her hair.

He kissed her properly, not the exhausted, grateful kiss on her cheek in the workshop, but with intention, his free hand against her jaw, and she kissed him back with the same straightforward honesty she brought to everything else she did.

The glass slippers had told them both the truth nearly a year ago. Now that he was kissing her, the shyness seemed ridiculous.

They worked together, ran the shop together. The idea of not having more with her was terrifying in the best possible way.

When they separated, she looked at him for a moment.

"You're going to be insufferable about this," she said.

"Probably," he agreed, smiling. “But I'm not going to be sad about it.”

“My mother will ask what took us so long. The glass slippers showed us each other long ago.”

“Hollis will say the same.” He stiffened. “He’ll say something like; you two were driving me crazy.”

She laughed, “Yes, he will.”

They both smiled and looked back at the frost garden, and her shoulder stayed against his, and neither of them went inside for a long while.

CHAPTER SEVEN

The Mine

The king's guards arrived at the estate before breakfast was cleared, four of them in Garrett's livery, travel-dusty and efficient. Aldric met them at the door. He had sent his own bird to the garrison the previous evening, before the woodpile, before the frost garden, before any of it. Whatever happened at the mine would be witnessed and recorded.

Neve had sent his bird to Garrett separately, a shorter message, three lines: *Sylvaine's argent mine needs an audit. Possible forged land council documents. Send someone with authority to open the books.*

Garrett's reply had come at first light, one line: *Already moving. Go with Aldric.*

Ilara came down to breakfast in riding clothes.

Aldric looked at her across the table.

"I know the layout," she said, in the tone that closed discussions. "And I want to see it in daylight. With guards."

Aldric nodded once and said nothing else.

Emory appeared in the doorway behind her, also in riding clothes.

Neve looked at him.

"I know the layout too," Emory said. "I found it when I went after Mother."

Ilara turned to look at her son. Then she looked at Aldric. Something passed between them that needed no words.

"No," Ilara said. Her voice was not unkind but it was not negotiable either. "You are not going back to that place."

"I went there before," Emory said.

"You did. And it cost you three days and a cursed hatchet." She pulled out the chair beside her. "Sit down. Eat something. When we return, you can hear everything."

"Mother."

"A mine run by a fairy-turned hag is not a place for children, and you are still a child, whatever the last week has made you feel." She met his eyes steadily. "Sit down, Emory. You know we love you, and don't give me that incredulous look. I am sorry, sweetheart. It's too dangerous for a boy, let alone one who is exhausted."

Emory looked at his father.

Aldric shook his head once. "Your mother is home one day. Do not make her spend it arguing with you."

Emory sat. He was not happy about it. His jaw seemed to file a silent formal objection while complying with the ruling.

They left Emory at the table with the housekeeper, two boiled eggs, and strict instructions to stay on the grounds.

The ride to the mine ran east through frozen fields and then along the boundary line itself, the marker stones visible at intervals through the thin winter scrub. Ilara rode without speaking. When the first marker came into view, she looked at it and then looked away, and did not look back.

The mine entrance was cut into a low hillside half a mile east of the boundary marker, framed in timber that needed replacing, a cart track running down from it through churned mud now frozen solid in the overnight frost. Two lanterns hung at the entrance, burned out. The cart that should have been moving ore sat empty and listing against the timber frame.

Nobody came out to meet them.

One of the guards went first. Then Ilara, without waiting to be invited. Then Neve and Mira, then Aldric, then the remaining guards.

The tunnel opened into a working chamber perhaps forty feet across, low-ceilinged, the walls carrying the grey-blue shimmer of magical-grade argent in the rock. Neve had seen that shimmer before in supplier samples, but never still in this raw state. It was unmistakable.

It was also mostly gone.

What remained was a thin vein running along the eastern wall, no wider than his hand in most places, pinching to nothing at the far end of the chamber. Someone had worked at it recently. The tool marks were fresh. But the yield from a vein that thin would be minimal, a few pounds of workable ore at best.

The foreman's tool room was off the main chamber, a low door, unlocked now. The locked box was on the top shelf where Ilara had said it would be. One of the guards brought it down.

It took Neve three minutes with a simple glass pick to open the lock. Inside was the ledger, and beneath it, a folded document with a land council seal.

He unfolded it.

The document listed the eastern boundary of Sylvaine's holdings as running forty acres past the actual marker, placing the boundary well into Aldric's land. The seal was genuine. The surveyor's signature was genuine. The date was three years old, predating the dispute, but not as old as the Regentry's deed from the king, granting noble status to their family nearly a hundred years ago.

But the vein sketch inked into the document's margin told the real story. It ran from the mine chamber, through the false boundary, and continued northeast into the hillside on Aldric's side of the line. Whoever had drawn it had been working from actual survey data. The richest section of the vein, marked with close cross-hatching, sat entirely within Aldric's land.

"She didn't want forty acres," Neve said. "She wanted what was under them."

Aldric took the document and looked at it for a long moment. His jaw tightened. He handed it to one of the guards without speaking.

"The ledger," Mira said.

Neve opened it. The first section was production records, yield by week, declining steadily over eighteen months as the accessible vein exhausted itself. The second section was purchases, bulk argent ore bought from a foreign supplier at significant cost, the entries marked with a symbol he didn't recognize at first.

He looked at it longer.

"She was buying it in to maintain the appearance of production," Mira said quietly, reading over his shoulder. "So her supply contracts held."

"And to keep the price stable," Neve said. "If her yield collapsed publicly, the market rate would shift." He turned a page. The third section was payments, names and amounts, one of them appearing monthly with a sum that matched nothing a foreman or surveyor would be paid.

He showed it to Aldric.

Aldric read the name. His expression went very still. "He sits on the land council," he said. "He has for twelve years."

Neve closed the ledger. "Garrett needs this today."

"Yes," Aldric said. "He does."

"He's going to want to move fast. I'll give this to one of his guards outside to messenger him. Let's find the workers and see what they have to say."

The workers were in a dormitory cut into the hillside behind the main chamber, eight of them, a mix of ages, sitting or standing with the blank stillness of exhaustion. When Ilara walked in, two of them stood immediately. She had been here with them. They knew her face.

“My Lady,” one of them said, nodding to her.

Aldric moved ahead, speaking plainly and straightforwardly, like a lord talking to hardworking men who deserve honest words.

"The woman who owned this mine is imprisoned. The land dispute is settled. You are free to go." He looked around the room. "Written passage documents, signed by the Duke of Silverneve's guards. Your back wages will be paid from her accounts under guild authority. Every coin owed. If you want to leave now, we can document you as you go so you'll be able to pick up your coin at the Fairy Godparent's guild in Silverneve once it's been sorted."

Nobody spoke for a moment.

Then a man near the back said, "All of it?"

"All of it," Aldric said. "To the day. To the largest gold crown. To the smallest copper crown."

Three of them wanted to go home. Ilara crossed the room to them before the guards could.

"Come with me," she said. "I know what they need from you and I can help you through it quickly." She looked back at Neve once, then led them out toward the guards at the entrance.

The remaining five stayed where they were.

Their spokesman was a broad man of about fifty with chalk dust in his hair and calloused hands. His blue eyes landed on Aldric and said, "The vein on your side of the line, My Lord. How rich is it?"

"I don't know yet," Aldric said, shaking his head and shrugging. "I know it's a significant amount, but I have only just discovered this, so I am not sure to what extent it's even workable."

"We know," another man said. "We worked on the survey. Sylvaine had us map it before she filed the false document." He folded his arms. "It's the richest argent deposit in this part of the realm. Magical grade through most of it. You'd need experienced men. For a proper and fair wage, My Lord, I think we could be convinced to stay."

Aldric looked at him for a long moment. "Honest wages. Guild rates. Safe working conditions and no cursed tools, ever, for any reason. All curse tools are to be handed in now. So, they can be safely disposed of."

The man looked at his four companions. Something passed between them.

“No need in worrying about that, My Lord,” One from the side said. “They all stopped working yesterday morning, but we can gather them up, just the same. As far as safety goes, it's a mine, sir. We will make it as safe as a mine can be.”

"I am Stone, that’s Peeble, Leelee, Wheeler, and Barmy...”

“Barney!” Someone shouted. “I only told you about a hundred times.”

“Yes, Barney. That’s right. When do we start, My Lord?" The blue-eyed man said.

“Well, the men with me are going to want to do an investigation. Once they have completed it and we get your wages sorted from here, I am going to need have a meeting out on the land to decide where to start.”

“We can help with that. It will give my crew and me something to do while the Duke is finishing up his investigation for the Crown.” He looked over his shoulder. “You lot, this way, guards need a chat about that hag.”

The three leaving workers filed past Neve on their way to Ilara. The last one paused at the tunnel entrance and set something down against the timber frame with a deliberate clunk. The other two did the same. Three iron picks, laid down in a row without being asked.

Neve looked at them. Then he looked at the argent twine still threaded through the handles, binding the curse into the iron the way Sylvaine's twine had bound the curse into his glass.

The twine on the picks caught the afternoon light and threw a faint gold glitter.

He went very still.

He had seen that shimmer before. Gold dust in the argent twine, exactly like the twine Sylvaine had laid on his counter the morning she commissioned the hatchet. She had told him it came from Ilara's wedding ring, melted and dusted down, a mother's protection bound into the material. He had believed her. But these picks carried the same gold dust, and no wedding ring had ever touched them. The gold was in the twine before it arrived. It was in the twine when she bought it. It had always been there.

The foreign argent had a contaminant in it that flowed curses better than the pure stuff that had once come from this mine.

He pulled out the small commission ledger he carried in his coat and wrote three words: *gold dust, twine, no-harm.*

Mira glanced at the ledger. "What are you adding?"

"A clause," he said. "For the contract, I need to commission from the Giftwright Guild. Any ward commission, any binding, any enchanted object leaving this workshop gets a no-harm declaration sworn over the argent twine before a single thread goes in." He closed the ledger. "If the twine already carries intent when it arrives, the declaration will show it. When the client fills out the form."

"That would have caught her."

"Yes," he said. "It would have. We just didn't know. It's probably why she drove all the way to our shop instead of one nearer to the Eastern District. And the EverBright shops wouldn't have had giftwrights skilled enough to be able to do it."

"I think that just speaks to the intent that she had to harm," Aldric said.

Neve nodded. Never again would he take a commission like that.

As late afternoon settled in, Neve and Mira were checking their borrowed horses when Stone came out of the tunnel mouth carrying a canvas sack, which he held out to Neve.

"Found this in the foreman's stores," he said. "Last of the magical grade from the original vein, before the bought-in stock started. It's the real thing. Eastern district argent, finest pull we ever got out of that face."

“Where is the foreman?” Neve took the sack. It was heavier than it looked, the canvas darkening slightly where the raw argent ore pressed against it, that faint blue-grey shimmer visible even through the weave.

“Who knows?” He shrugged. "Foreman was keeping it for himself. It should go somewhere useful, like the person who was tricked into making that mad hatchet but also made that fairy star to free us. Should be more than enough out of the hag's stock to cover the cost of the star. I have heard they're expensive."

Enough for a year's worth of twine, at least. Maybe more.

“Runoff. Looks like he only took his gold with him.” Stone shrugged. “Probably for the best. Peeble would have pummeled him without the hag’s protection. He was out of here as soon as that paper bird from the Fairy Godparents arrived. Didn’t even read it.”

"Thank you," Neve said, patting the sack. “I know just what to do with it.” They could finally replace the last of the defective EverBright ornaments with it.

By the time Stone went back inside, the winter light had shifted to the flat gold of late afternoon. Neve looked at the angle of it against the hillside and calculated the ride back.

"We need to go," he said to Mira. "Hollis has been with Garrett's maid since yesterday."

She nodded. “I am not sure who to feel sorry for. Hollis isn’t used to being waited on.”

"Yes," he said. "From the ground up. This is sort of yours, though. You made the fairy star." He patted the argent.

"We, together, will do some good with it. I want to finish the ornaments."

He smiled. "Great minds think alike."

"Do you know how to process it into Argent Twine?" Mira asked. "Because I don't have a clue."

"I'm about to figure it out. I have read books on it, back when Hollis and I were fighting over the pitiful argent twine EverBright was supplying us. Although if this was the state of the supply, I can see how they were trying to stretch it out."

Aldric and Ilara were still with the guards near the entrance, the ledger open between them, and one of Garrett's men making notes. Aldric looked up when Neve raised a hand and nodded once. Ilara met Neve's eyes across the yard and gave him the same decisive nod she had given him at the gate the day before.

It was enough. He helped Mira onto her horse, then got on his own.

He looked back once at the mine entrance, at the exhausted vein, the empty carts, and the tool marks on the chamber walls, then turned his horse toward the road and did not look back again.

Neve tied the sack to his saddle and turned his horse toward the road. Mira fell in beside him. The mine entrance shrank behind them as they crested the cart track, and then the beech wood closed around the road. There was only the cold air, the sound of hooves on frozen ground, and the light going thin and grey ahead of them.

Hollis was in his chair when they came through the workshop door, hands folded, tea at his elbow. The maid Garrett had sent was visible through the office door, moving quietly.

His eyes went to Neve's face. Then to Mira. Then back to Neve.

He said nothing.

He picked up his tea.

The furnace had been banked low overnight and needed building up. Neve set the coat with the shards over the back of the stool and began to work the bellows. Mira hung her coat on the hook by the door and picked up her sketchbook.

The workshop smelled of argent twine and cooling glass.

After a while, Hollis said, "Good. It's about time. You two were driving me insane."

He did not specify what he meant.

Both Mira and Neve cast shy looks at each other before getting back to work processing the argent into argent twine. A large book lay open between them as they read how to process the argent potions into the twine.

Also by

Enter the *Giftwright*
Workshop
A reader community for Karine Green's Giftwright
Tales

In Silverneve, magic is not cast. It is made, folded into glass, woven through argent twine, anchored to the people who need it most. Join the workshop list for news about the series, behind-the-scenes craft notes, and first access to new releases.

email list sign up: https://stauntonpress.blog/2026/04/30/enter-the-giftwright-workshop/

https://stauntonpress.blog/

Don't forget to review

Reviews are the argent twine for author careers. They hold everything together and make the next book possible. If you enjoyed The Glass Hatchet, a short review on Amazon or Goodreads would mean more than you know.

Book One

Book Two

Book Three

Book Five— Coming soon.

About the author

Karine Green writes fantasy and paranormal romances with cunning heroines/heroes who face internal and external foes. In real life, Karine is a retired emergency services worker with experience in two major cities. She now works as an English as a Second Language teacher.

Writing and storytelling has always been a passion for Karine. She would get in trouble in English class for "embellishing" English assignments to be more interesting. She grew up north of Detroit and worked in Nashville. Upon retiring she now calls Tampa home. She loves retirement since she can now write full-time.

Her favorite way to combat writer's block is to watch the news. The news always provides inspiration for stories that can be embellished into amazing stories. It even provides names that can be mixed and matched into believable characters.

Find out more about her books Here

www.ingramcontent.com/pod-product-compliance
Lightning Source LLC
La Vergne TN
LVHW051010080826
845145LV00009B/2548